LOVE BIG

A Mythological Fable About How to Be the Hero of Your Story

KAT KRONENBERG

illustrated by David Miles

GREENLEAF
BOOK GROUP PRESS

Ancient myths say we are all born with the wondrous gift of stardust in our hearts. Read, discover, and try the animal's second secret—shhh—to light your heart of stars and become the hero of your stories together!

In the wilds of East Africa, hundreds of years had passed since the savannas began. The land was dry and desolate with animals so hungry and mean that they had stopped believing in their dreams. Until . . . this moody Baboon discovered a new powerful secret—SHHH—

3

It began one afternoon when rude Rhino was desperately racing to eat a new patch of green grass, snorting, "MOVE, you stinky beetle! I'm starving!"

But BAM! WHACK!

Rhino smacked his rump with a bump to avoid
a pile of poop, snorting, "Gross! You live in poop!
You stink, Beetle! You did this!"

Bossy Baboon heard and couldn't help but sneer,
"Wa-Hu-Wa-Hu-Wa-You bully. Don't blame Beetle.
You tripped."

"So?" whined Rhino, rubbing his rump in pain.
"It's still that stinky beetle's fault."

Beetle took a thoughtful breath and rolled the cure-all mud ball he
made to Rhino stuttering nervously, "T-t-try this. It helps with the pain.
Plus, I-I think you're really cool, Rhinoceros!"

Surprised by Beetle's kindness, Rhino tried the cure-all ball. It worked!
So, with a horn beginning to grow, Rhino gave Beetle a bump, saying,
"Thanks, dude! That was really *cool* of you."

They shared big smiles. Then bumped and clapped together,
"WE believe! WE can—"

11

YES! Rhino fixed the Termite's crashed castle, helped Baboon hollow his drum, and gave Beetle his yummy, new snack-from-a-stick, saying, "Dude, thanks to you, I know *to make a point to be kind any time my whiny-bully-bound-power-pout hangs out!* The ROCKIN' HORNS I just grew prove real COOLNESS happens if I do!"*

* Rhinoceroses have a prehensile upper lip that hangs out like a power-pout, which displays their rude, whiny way. They also grow horns that are believed to have special properties.

Excited, the next afternoon, Baboon had just started playing his drum when he heard Mad Mamma Hare scold, "You need to share your snack."

In trouble, Little Hare mumbled, "Fine. I'll go find my own food."

She left, and her mom cried out,
"Please stay, my sweet Little Hare.
It's gonna get cold." But Little Hare
kept walking as clouds filled the sky.

Freezing and starving, Little Hare walked by
nosy Baboon, who sneered, "Wa-Hu-Wa-Hu-
Wa-Your mom warned you."

"So?" snapped Little Hare stubbornly, hiding her face,
shivering cold, alone, and afraid.

Rhino took a thoughtful breath and gave Little Hare his flattened mud
ball, saying, "Get warm with this make-do mud cape, and dude, take
my new snack-from-a-stick. It's d-e-licious!"

"Cool cape! I mean, WARM cape." Little Hare laughed at her joke with her very first Hare hop. "Beetle's right. You are *cool*!"

They shared big smiles. Then hopped and clapped together, "WE believe! WE can—"

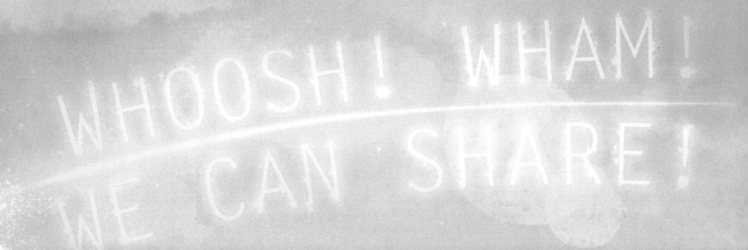

YES! Little Hare went home to share her new snack-on-a-stick with her siblings. They had so much fun that they learned to *HOP*, *ZIP*, *POP*, and *SKIP*—the skills their family needed to survive! Happy, all their ears went up, and they celebrated with a song:

Hop! Pop! Hip bump!
SHARE and LOVE BIG!
IT'S A DREAM-TASTIC
WAY TO LIVE!*

* Hares use their ears to communicate, and they get away from danger by hopping and popping in the air with a zig zag pattern.

21

The next afternoon, curious Baboon quietly asked Little Hare, "What do I do? I want my dream to come true too." Suddenly, the ground shook under his bum.

Bright-eyed, Baboon saw why! Two Lionesses were racing and roaring, "Stop that Lion!" "He stole our snack!"

Running scared, hungry Lion crashed into Little Hare. BAM!

Baboon sneered, "Wa-Hu-Wa-Hu-Wa-Hurry Lion! Get up! They're coming after you!"

"So?" Lion cried, terrified, and scrambled to
his feet, starving. "They didn't listen when I asked.
So, I stole their snack!"

Little Hare took a thoughtful breath and looked Lion
in the eye, saying, "I understand! But I just learned it's
hoppier to share. So, maybe try that?"

Lion, with a mane beginning to grow, forgot he was in danger.
He was too busy smiling at Little Hare, saying,
"No one's ever listened to me before or helped me see what I need to . . ."

"R-R-R-O-A-R-R!" The lionesses attacked—

WHACK!

SMACK!

BOOM!

HOME
FoR SALE
FREE

KAPOW!
Ow! OO!

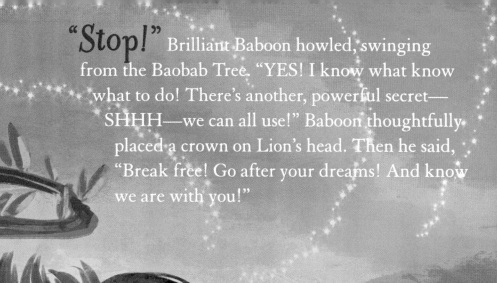

"*Stop!*" Brilliant Baboon howled, swinging from the Baobab Tree. "YES! I know what know what to do! There's another, powerful secret— SHHH—we can all use!" Baboon thoughtfully placed a crown on Lion's head. Then he said, "Break free! Go after your dreams! And know we are with you!"

Lion broke free! Baboon and he shared big smiles and clapped together, "WE believe! WE can—"

YES! Lion gave back the stolen snack, apologizing as his brilliant mane blew in the breeze. Then he declared, "WE must share!" As they all ate, Lion listened, helping the Lionesses with their problems. Grateful, they crowned Lion the very first *King of the Beasts*.

To celebrate, Baboon passed out his pompoms and drums, as Lion roared loud and proud in his new crown, "Take *pride*! Take time to hear with both ears, so you, too, can be a leader . . . "*

But Lion stopped mid-celebration—

* Lions have become the dominant animal on the savanna with their ability to lead, intense social pride, courageous attitude, royal look, and commanding roar!

33

—because Little Hare squeaked, "Pee-ew! What stinks?!"

"It's me-me," stuttered Beetle nervously, embarrassed by
the poop ball he was rolling to Lion. "My-my home IS this
stinky poop. What *do* I *do*-do?"

Everyone laughed, "Aa . . . Ee . . . Ii . . . Oo . . . Uu-u,"
thinking Beetle had made a doo-doo joke.

But Beetle's feelings were so hurt that he quickly hid.
To help with his do-do dilemma, Lion got Baboon, and
together they wrote Beetle a song. Sing along:

*Twinkle, twinkle, share a smile
Lights up stardust all the while
Dance "We can" and dare Believe
Loving big we all succeed
Twinkle, twinkle, hearts of stars
Guiding us we will go far

* Lion and Baboon's song is sung to the tune of "Twinkle, Twinkle, Little Star." Sing along!

After the song, Lion looked Beetle in the eye and declared with his royal ROAR, "Since you first dared to care, we've learned to LOVE BIG, working together to achieve our dreams. We thank you."

Beetle's SMILE was huge as they all shared
big smiles. Then they clapped together,
"WE believe! WE can—"

WHOOSH! WHAM!
WE CAN CARE!

"**YES!** Beetle, you're our hero!" Everyone cheered.
"Look! Your *poop balls of fertilized-fun* spread everywhere,
are turning the savanna green, so now we can eat!"

42

Beetle flip-flopped on top of his poop ball, dancing, "YES! If someone as miserable as me, with the help of a WE can transform my *do-do* dilemna into something grand, WE all can! So please, try the secret—SHHH! LOVE big! Share a SMILE and together, BELIEVE!*

* Dung Beetles are heroically vital to an ecosystem! They turn animal dung into balls that help sanitize and fertilize the land for food and so much more.

43

With that, the newfound friends put up their *Happy-Hoppy Ears*, and celebrated with Baboon's dream, his Boom Shake Celebration:

Wa-Whoo!
Shake your pompoms,
Share big smiles,
With hearts of stars lit
We can all go miles

NOTES FOR TWO-LEGGERS OF ALL AGES:

–SHHH–

Study these fascinating animals on Kat's website. We can learn so much from their lives. Plus, the Second Secret they use is so powerful that Baby Baboon wants to make sure we understand these important keys to their discovery—

★ Stars are scientifically proven to live above us, within us, and around us all. The stars surrounding us always twinkle, reminding us that we are all born extraordinary, that—

★ We have hearts of stars: star-stuff hidden in our chests just waiting to be lit.

★ To light this priceless, timeless treasure hidden in our chests, we must **SMILE & BELIEVE.** The African Animals call it catching CATCH-M.

CATCH-M is the name of our big, marvelous, shared smile that invites the star dust that surrounds us to WHOOSH into our lives and WHAM ignite through shared belief the gift of stars in our hearts.

Baby Baboon came up with this catchy nickname to remind us that we too can light our heart of stars, giving us the courage we need to achieve our wildest DREAMS. She also has some fun things we can do alone, with family, friends, or in the classroom to prepare to catch CATCH-M too-gather!

(Share your fun with our LIVE BIG COMMUNITY using a #LiveBig #CatchM on social media.)

"We are made of star-stuff. There are pieces of star within us all . . . Every one of us is, in the cosmic perspective, precious."—Carl Sagan

1. Create Your Own CATCH-M

"Never underestimate the power of a smile which has the potential to turn a life around."—Leo Buscaglia

Take time to draw your smile, a BIG SMILE that comes all the way up from your belly, through your chest, & shines from your face who you are! Use your smile to remind you of the stars that surround you and are in you, so you can have fun sharing smiles and become the hero of your story too.

Take your drawn smile on a CATCH-M ADVENTURE: on a trip, to school, or wherever you choose. On your adventure, build a LIVE BIG CLUB, as you remind others to celebrate their smiles too! Then find as many ways in a day to catch CATCH-M together, take pictures as you do, & journal too—remembering to share a big **SMILE BUILDS FORTUNE-FILLED TREASURE CHESTS** for all!

"Shoot for the stars! LOVE BIG! Love the life that you live, and be thankful for every breath that it gives."—Jaxon Reed Kronenberg

2. Make a Rhino Party Hat—with Your Own Kindness Pact

"Kindness is the opportunity we have every day to change the world."—RAKtivist

Be like Rhino with his horn! Make a POINT to remind yourself everyday that **KIND IS COOL!** Start by making a real point in your life, A *RHINO PACT PARTY HAT*:

A. Decorate a piece of paper, even adding your **CATCH-M.**

B. Roll the paper into a HORN-SHAPED POINT like a cone. Either tape or staple it together.

C. Wear your Rhino Horn like a party hat. Celebrate that KIND is cool! Even make your own **KINDNESS PACT—TO FIND WAYS EVERY DAY to be KIND.**

For community building fun, gather your—**LIVE BIG CLUB**! Make a KINDNESS PACT together by creating and decorating an AP-POINT-ED LOVE CAN— a can, a jar, a bucket, or anything. Every day make sure everyone in the Club fills the container with their act of kindness for the day!

Have a party and celebrate your Club's commitment to fill the LOVE CAN daily by remembering the Rhino Horn. Since these horns are made of the same stuff as our hair, during the party, have everyone make a pledge to the Club's KINDNESS PACT by filling the AP-POINT-ED LOVE CAN with a strand of their hair. If that's too weird—no problem—just draw your CATCH-M with hair on a rock, a bead, a marble, or paper to place at the base of the LOVE CAN. Once placed, know you are part of a LIVE BIG CLUB who wants to live their best life together and make a POINT to be kind to everybody every day.

Display THE AP-POINT-ED LOVE CAN for all to see, celebrate, & remember that A CLUB OF KIND KIDS CREATES COOL.

3. Design Hare's Cape—With Your Own Coat of Arms

"Be a rainbow in someone else's cloud."—Maya Angelou

Be like Hare and gather your LIVE BIG CLUB! Together, make a **HAPPY, HOPPY, HERALDIC DESIG** that shows the club's goals, achievements, mottos, location, or anything else to help inspire **CONNECTION, COMMUNICATION, & CONTRIBUTION.** Create your own or use "The Coat of Arms Download" on Kat's website.

For community building fun, place your COAT OF ARMS on capes! Celebrate and go out like SUPERHEROES! Catch CATCH-M together by finding ways every day as a group to be kind, share, listen, and care! The group experience creates CRASH-N-DROVE PRIDE! *CRASH* is a group of Rhinos, *DROVE* is Hare & *PRIDE* is Lions! Baby Baboon came up with this FUN PUNNY name to remind us—An odd club can come to gather to create a heroic **RE-EVOL-UTION!**

Display your club's **COAT OF ARMS** prominently to celebrate **THE STRENGTH & CONNECTION OF YOUR LIVE BIG CLUB.** Also, download the "LOVE BIG GRAM," a free APP on the homepage of Ka website, to share your coat of arms & encourage others to LOVE BIG too!

"A deep sense of love and belonging is an irreducible need of all people.
We are biographically, cognitively, physically, and spiritually wired to love,
to be loved, and to belong."—Brené Brown

4. Craft Lion's Crown—Honor Your Own Life

"Crowns aren't made of rhinestones. They are made of discipline, determination, and a hard-to-find jewel called courage."—Susan Albers Kennedy

Be like Lion! Know you are a KING—or a QUEEN— and born extraordinary! The only you who will ever be! Tap into your possibility! Celebrate your gifts, talents, & dreams. Learn to be a true LEADER by LISTENING to who you are and by LISTENING to others, & lead a ROYAL-REVERED-REVOLUTIONARY LIFE! Craft & wear your own crown with complete pride, or use "The Crown Download" on Kat's website.

For community building fun, Baby Baboon wants you to gather **your LIVE BIG CLUB!** Every day, week, or month, CROWN a different person. The ONE WEARING THE CROWN gets to:

★ **LEAD** the group.

★ Enjoy **SHOW & TELL!** A time for the crowned honoree to talk about their passion—their favorite book, toy, sport, musical instrument, art, hero, etc. This time offers your club a way to honor one another by **LISTENING & SHARING** in each other's gifts, talents, dreams, & build a stronger **WE**.

   (Lion says, "Listen twice as much as we speak. It's why we all have two ears & one mouth.")

★ Celebrate with a **GIVE-AWAY**, a timeless African Animal tradition. The crowned honoree creates a ritual where they give away something they love, treasure, or find useful with a surrendered & joyful heart. It's a sign they are willing to **SHARE**, sacrifice, & celebrate the power of their **WE**. The animals believe sacrifice means "to make sacred," so the act of giving allows their club to know no one will ever be abandoned, orphaned, or left without food, dwelling, or help. The gift of giving is an HONORED way to celebrate your club's willingness to THRIVE & LIVE in A-BUN-DANCE TOGETHER

5. Termite Tricks to Encourage—Plus, Dung Beetle's Do-Do Game & More

To learn "What DO you DO?" in tough times, play Dung Beetle's Do-Do Game in the Fun section on Kat's website, or write your own stories using The Hero's Journey in the Learn section. For more fun, solve the Termite Tricks below & use them to create your own:

★ Page 13: Termites have the letters "E" "K-N" on their backs to remind us that . . . ?

★ Page 21: Termites wrote the letters "B" "A" & "E" like a Coat of Arms on Hare's Cape displayed at her home to encourage & remind everyone to . . . ?

★ Page 22 and 33: Termites used sticks to show us how easy it is to "Flip ME to . . . ?

★ Page 37: Termites used sticks to also show us that "LOVE can start and be part of a . . . ?"

★ Page 38: Termites & Dung Beetle have the letters "C-L-8" "E" on their backs to say . . . ?

★ Page 43: Termites arranged the letters "E" "R" & the number "1" for fun to remind us to . . . ?

★ Page 48: For one funny last bit of encouragement, Termites gathered together on the last page with the letters "E" "S" "B-U-T" to say . . . ?

(Answers: P. 13—We Can; P. 21—Be a WE; PP. 22 & 33—Flip ME to WE; P. 37—LOVE can start & be part of a revolution; P. 38—Celebrate WE; P. 43—Smile - WE Are One; P. 48—WE is Beauty)

To celebrate LOVE, *find more fun*, see some Crowns & Capes, or play Dung Beetle's "DoDo Game," visit Kat's website: www.katkronenberg.com.

Now it's your turn! Go! Enjoy one another and try the—SHHH—secret too! There's no telling what we can do!

Close your eyes.
Take three deep breaths.
Love BIG!
Be kind.
Share.
Listen.
Care.
SMILE big together.
Clap, "WE BELIEVE! WE CAN!"
And—Whoosh! Wham!
WE can . . .

(The proceeds from *Love Big* will go to support other Two-Leggers' dreams as we celebrate the magic and marvel of WE:

www.we.org, www.grameenamerica.org, & www.donorschoose.org.)

"A smile is a U-SHAPED BRIDGE that can connect us to everything—our head to our heart, **our lives to one another,** & our dreams to the power of something GREATER! So go catch CATCH-M too-gather, celebrate the great things WE can do, & let your life shine!"
—Kat Kronenberg

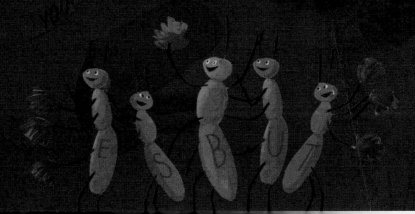

Made in the USA
Middletown, DE
19 December 2023

46374716R00029